OTTO'S
BACKWARDs DAY

FRANK CAMMUSO

with JAY LYNCH

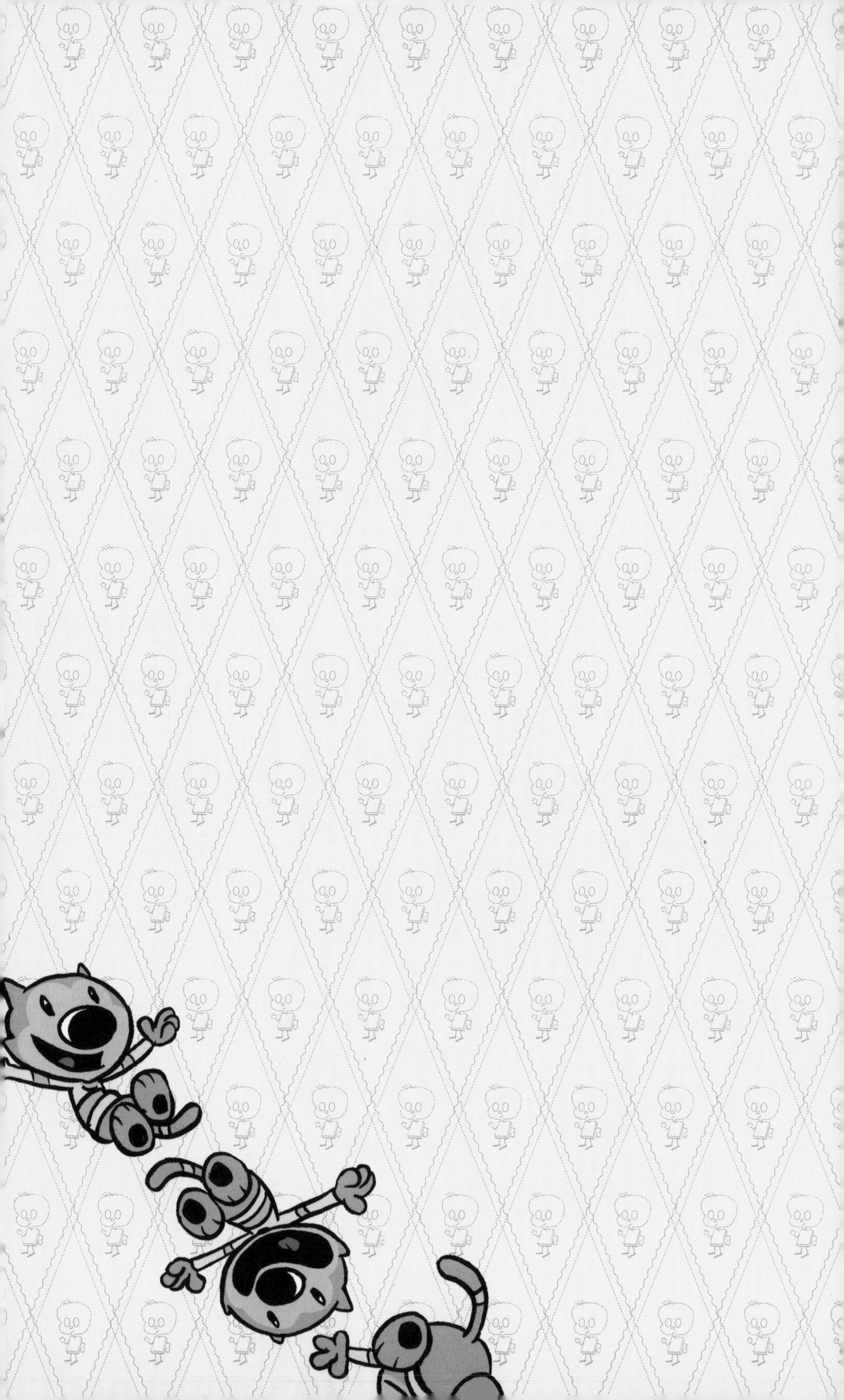

OTTO'S
BACKWARDS DAY

A TOON BOOK BY

FRANK CAMMUSO
with **JAY LYNCH**

TOON BOOKS IS AN IMPRINT OF CANDLEWICK PRESS

A JUNIOR LIBRARY GUILD SELECTION

Also look for Otto's Orange Day, by the same authors.

For Khai

Editorial Director: FRANÇOISE MOULY

Book Design: FRANÇOISE MOULY & JONATHAN BENNETT

FRANK CAMMUSO'S artwork was drawn in india ink and colored digitally.

CHILDREN'S DEPARTMENT
Falmouth Public Library
300 Main Street
Falmouth, MA 02540

A TOON Book™ © 2013 RAW Junior, LLC, 27 Greene Street, New York, NY 10013. TOON Books® is an imprint of Candlewick Press, 99 Dover Street, Somerville, MA 02144. No part of this book may be used or reproduced in any manner whatsoever without written permission except in the case of brief quotations embodied in critical articles and reviews. TOON Books®, LITTLE LIT® and TOON Into Reading™ are trademarks of RAW Junior, LLC. All rights reserved. Printed in Johor Bahru, Malaysia by Tien Wah Press (Pte.) Ltd.

Library of Congress Cataloging-in-Publication Data:

Cammuso, Frank, author, illustrator.

Otto's backwards day : a TOON book / by Frank Cammuso with Jay Lynch.

pages cm. – (Easy-to-read comics. Level 3)

Summary: "Someone stole Otto's birthday! When Otto the cat and his robot sidekick Toot follow the crook, they discover a topsy-turvy world where rats chase cats and people wear underpants over their clothes"– Provided by publisher.

ISBN 978-1-935179-33-7 (alk. paper)

1. Graphic novels. [1. Graphic novels. 2. Birthdays–Fiction. 3. Cats–Fiction. 4. Humorous stories.] I. Lynch, Jay, author. II. Title.

PZ7.7.C36Or 2013   741.5'973–dc23   2012047661

ISBN 13: 978-1-935179-33-7 ISBN 10: 1-935179-33-0

13 14 15 16 17 18 TWP 10 9 8 7 6 5 4 3 2 1

WWW.TOON-BOOKS.COM

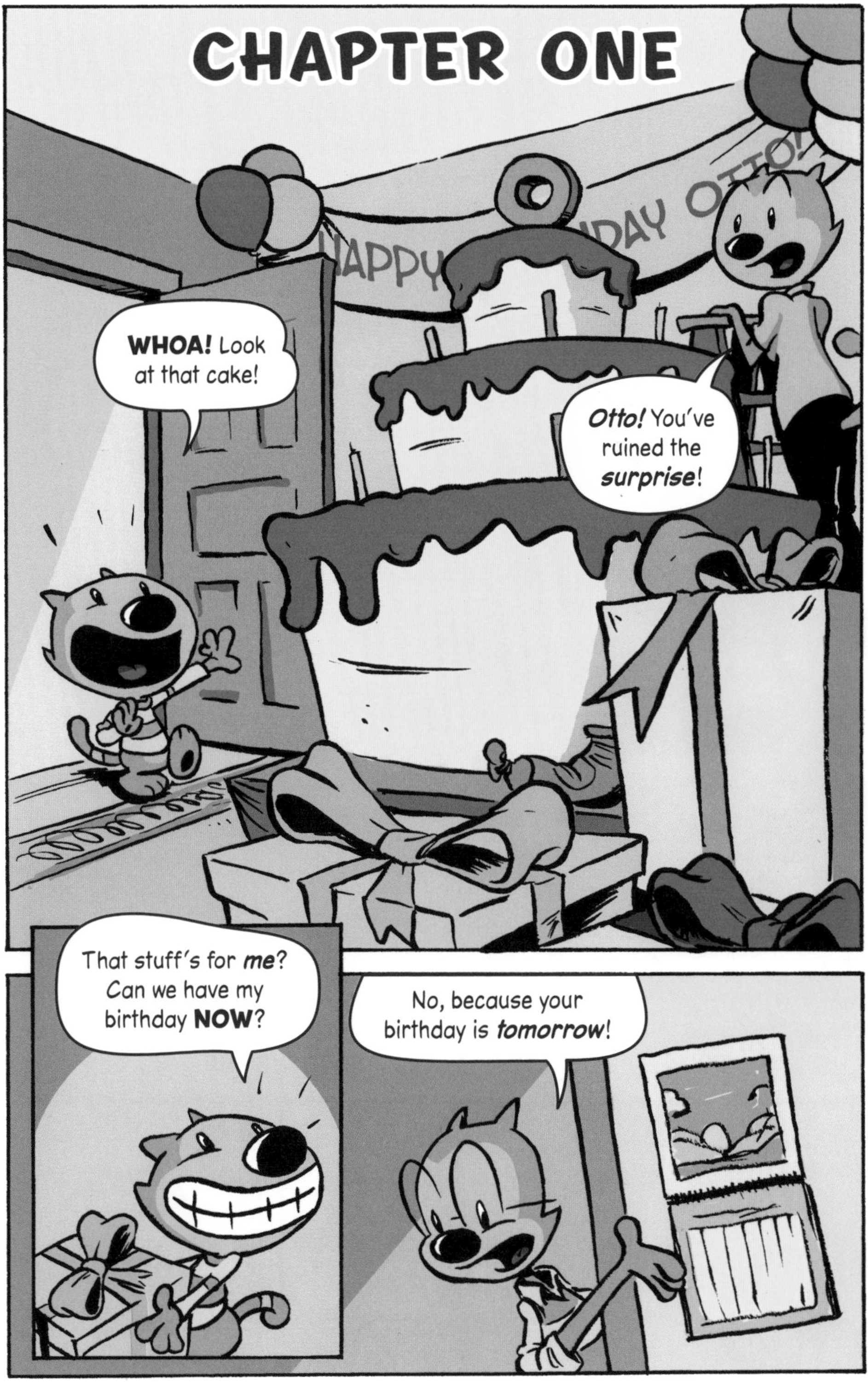
CHAPTER ONE
HAPPY DAY OTTO!
WHOA! Look at that cake!
Otto! You've ruined the surprise!
That stuff's for me? Can we have my birthday NOW?
No, because your birthday is tomorrow!

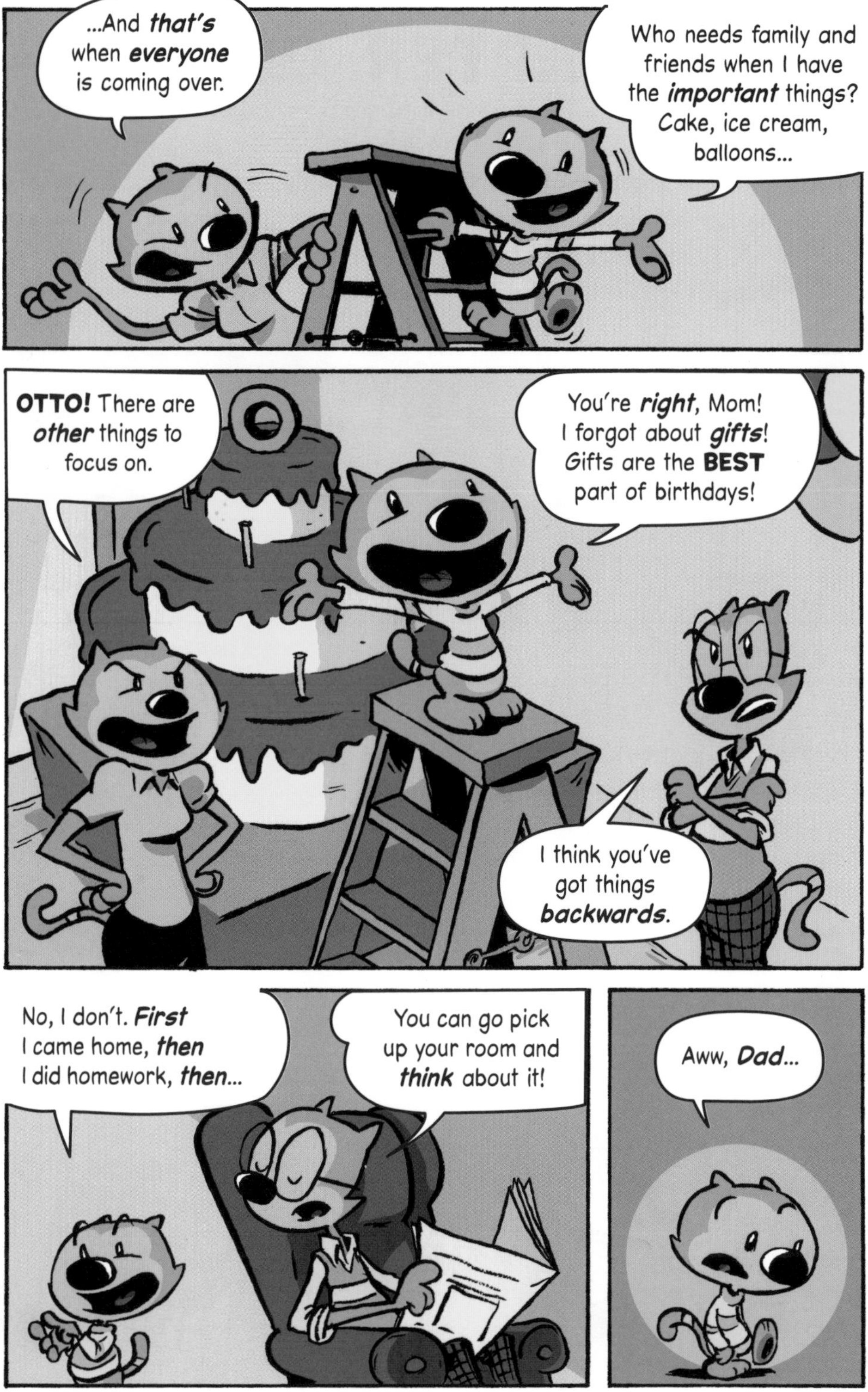
...And *that's* when *everyone* is coming over.
Who needs family and friends when I have the *important* things? Cake, ice cream, balloons...
OTTO! There are *other* things to focus on.
You're *right*, Mom! I forgot about *gifts*! Gifts are the **BEST** part of birthdays!
I think you've got things *backwards*.
No, I don't. *First* I came home, *then* I did homework, *then*...
You can go pick up your room and *think* about it!
Aww, *Dad*...

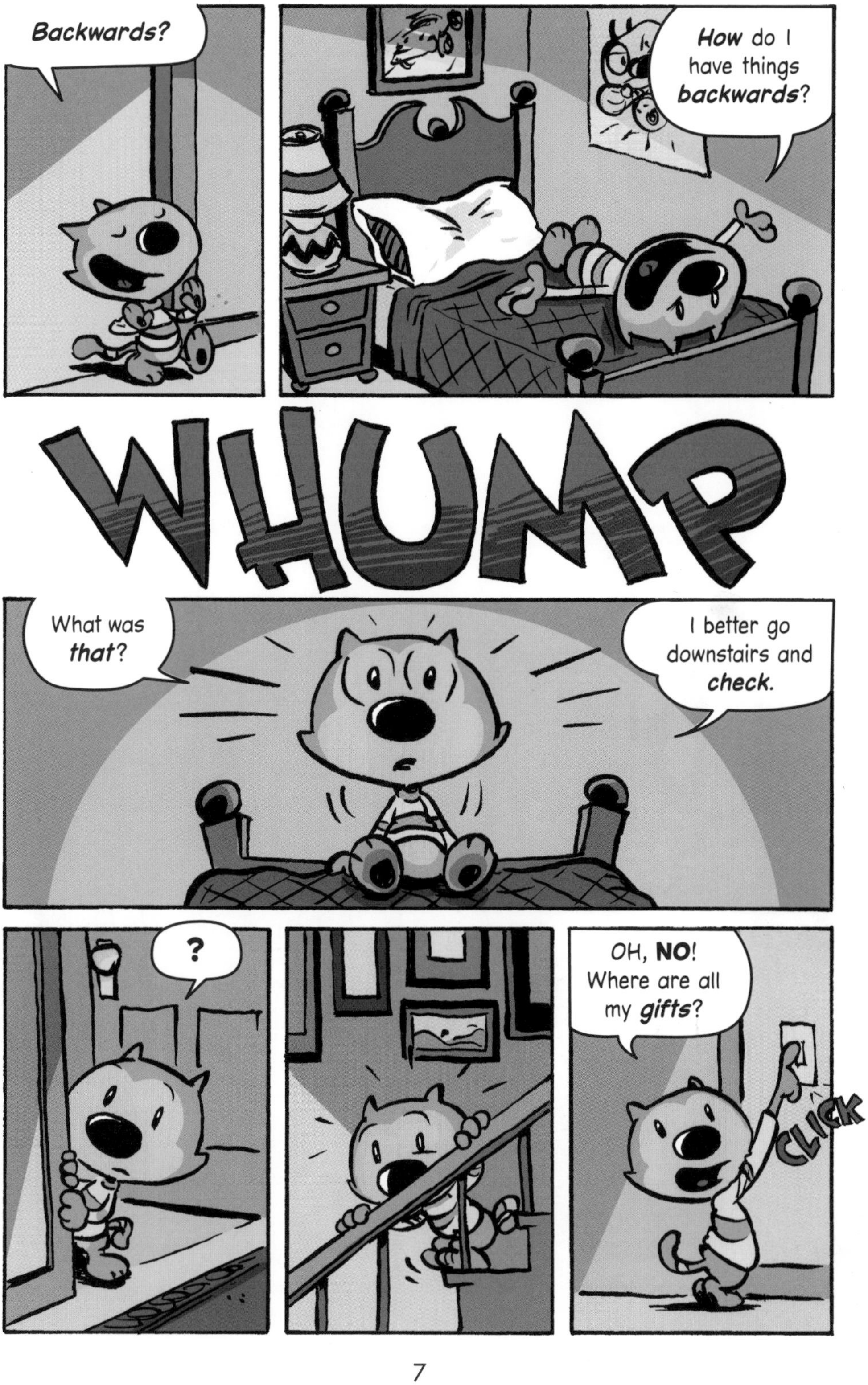
Backwards?
How do I have things backwards?
WHUMP
What was that?
I better go downstairs and check.
?
OH, NO! Where are all my gifts?
CLICK

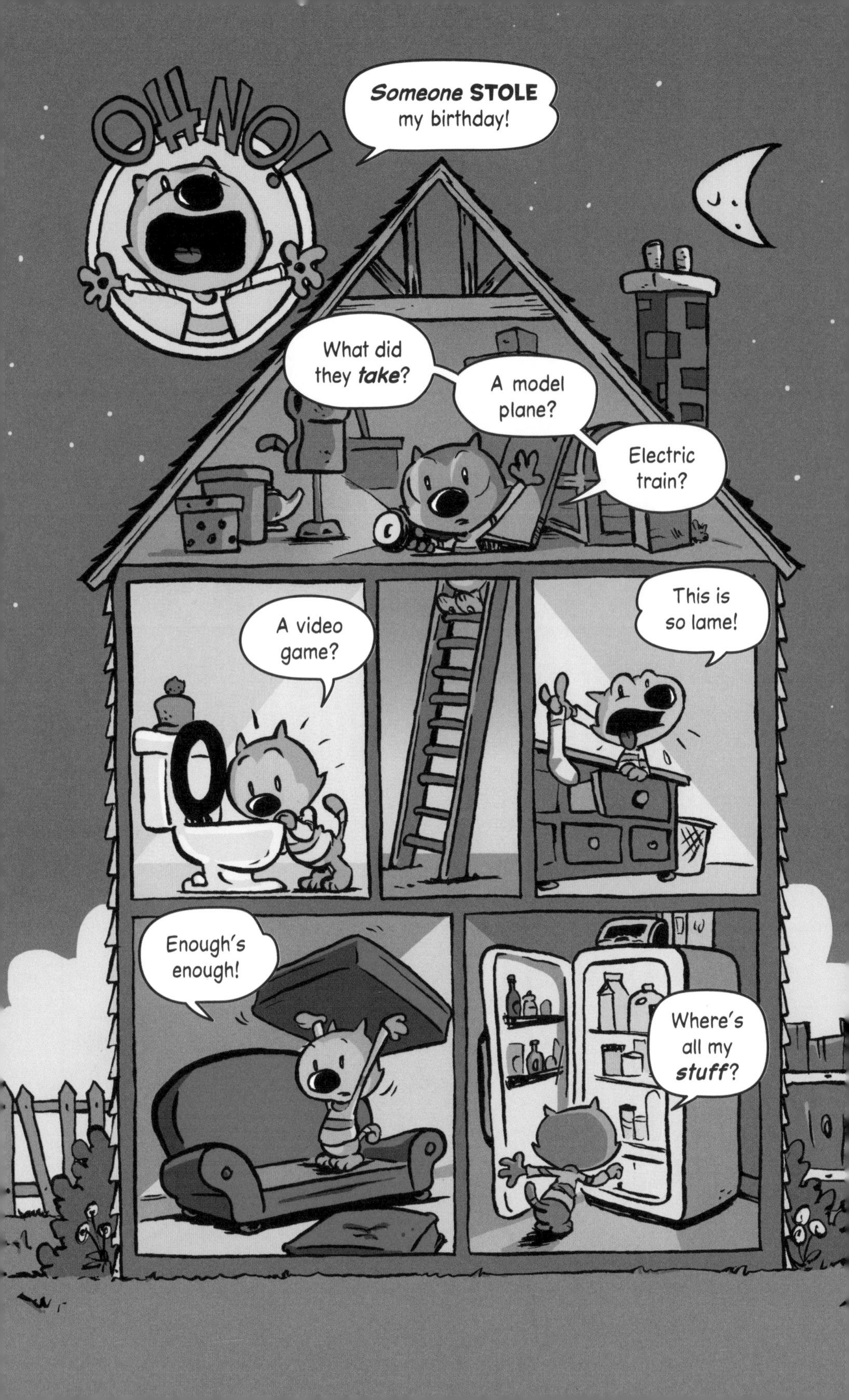
OH NO!
Someone **STOLE** my birthday!
What did they ***take***?
A model plane?
Electric train?
A video game?
This is so lame!
Enough's enough!
Where's all my ***stuff***?

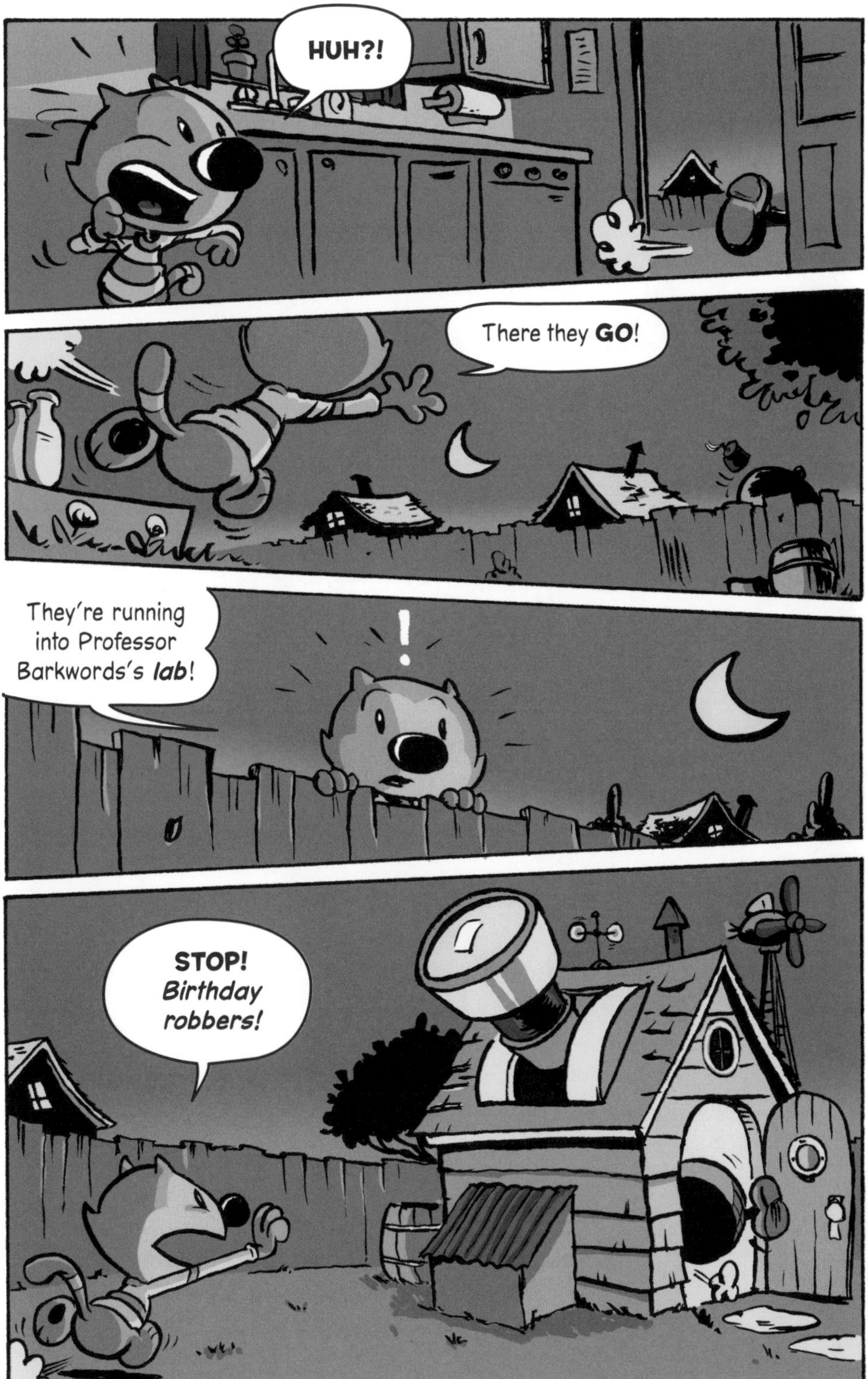
HUH?!
There they GO!
They're running into Professor Barkwords's lab!
STOP! Birthday robbers!

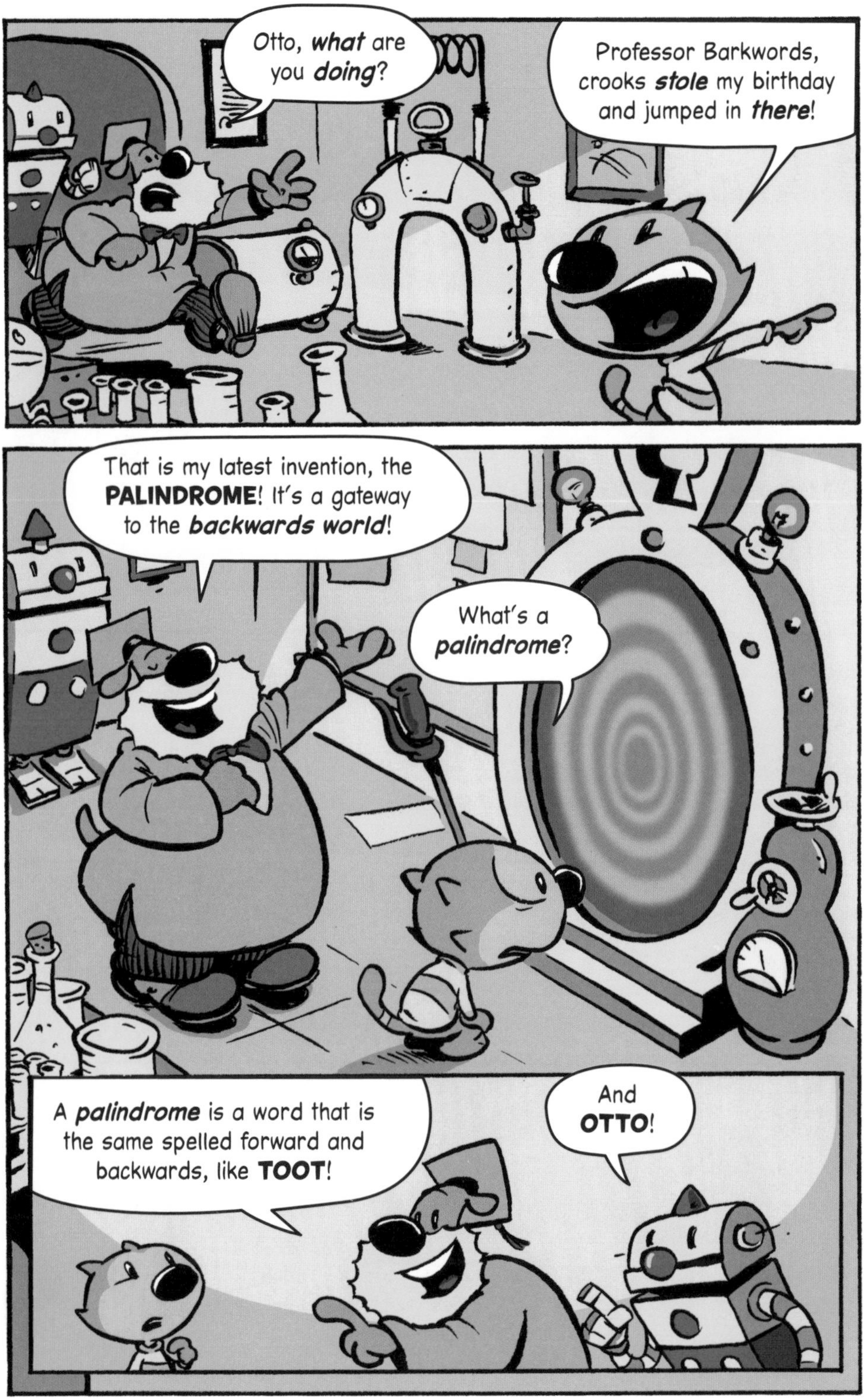
Otto, *what* are you *doing*?
Professor Barkwords, crooks *stole* my birthday and jumped in *there*!
That is my latest invention, the **PALINDROME**! It's a gateway to the *backwards world*!
What's a *palindrome*?
A *palindrome* is a word that is the same spelled forward and backwards, like **TOOT**!
And **OTTO**!

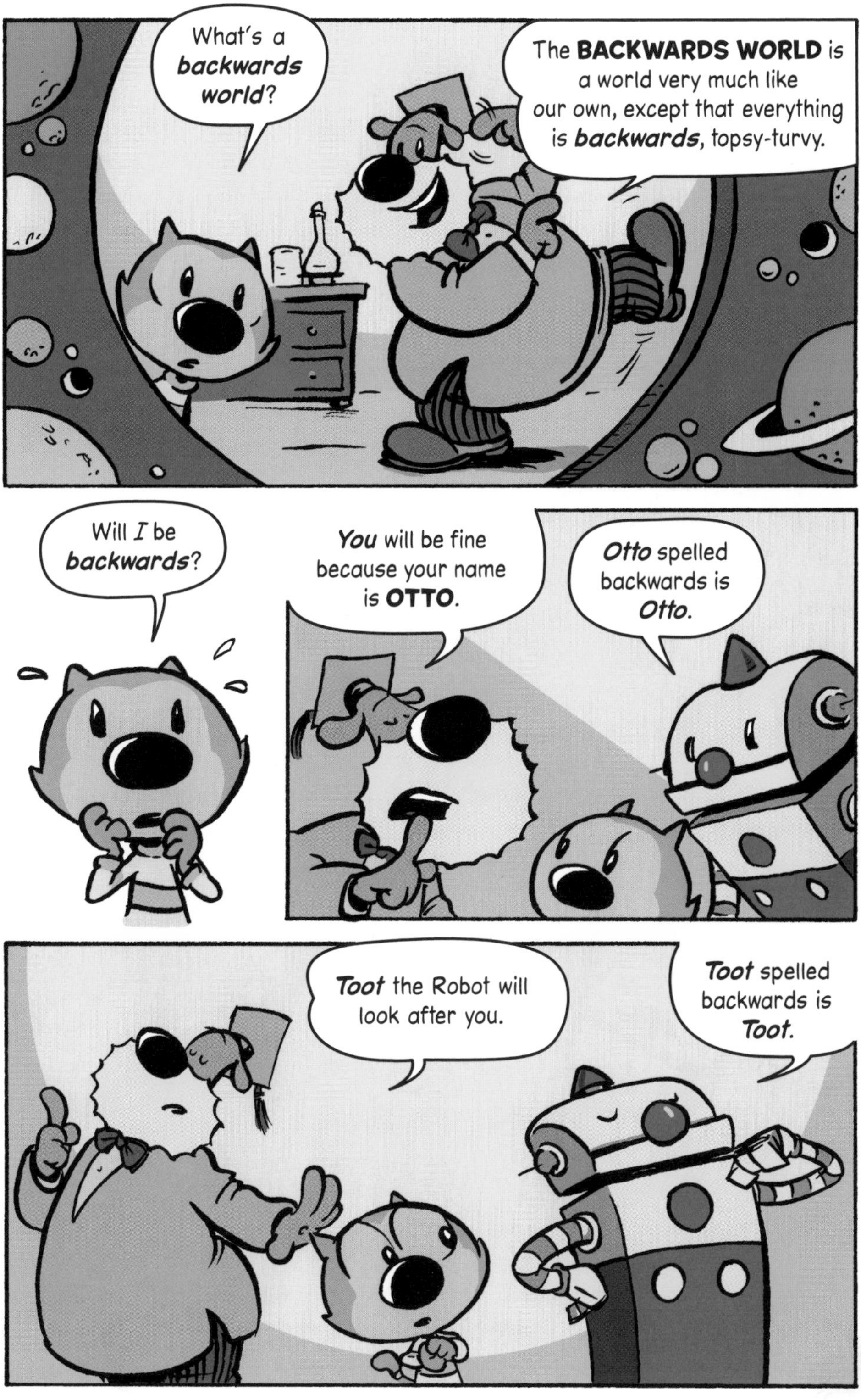
What's a *backwards world*?
The **BACKWARDS WORLD** is a world very much like our own, except that everything is ***backwards***, topsy-turvy.
Will *I* be ***backwards***?
You will be fine because your name is **OTTO**.
Otto spelled backwards is *Otto*.
Toot the Robot will look after you.
Toot spelled backwards is *Toot*.

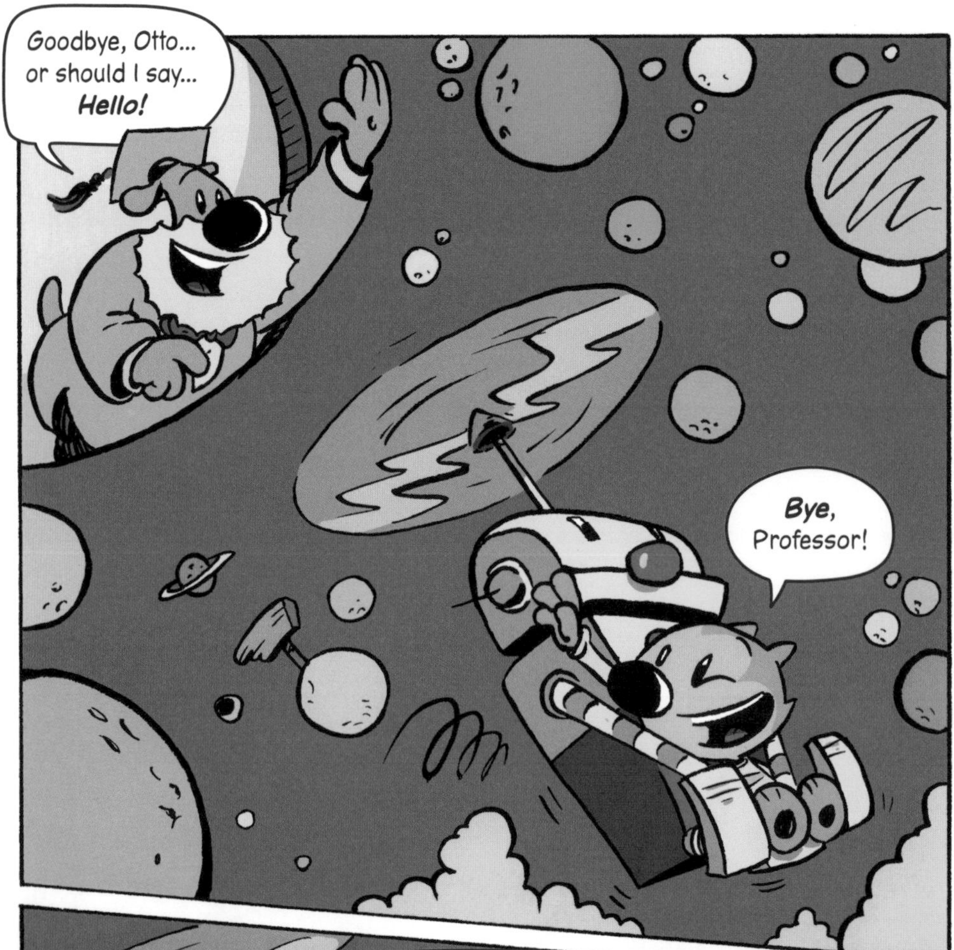
Goodbye, Otto...
or should I say...
Hello!
Bye,
Professor!

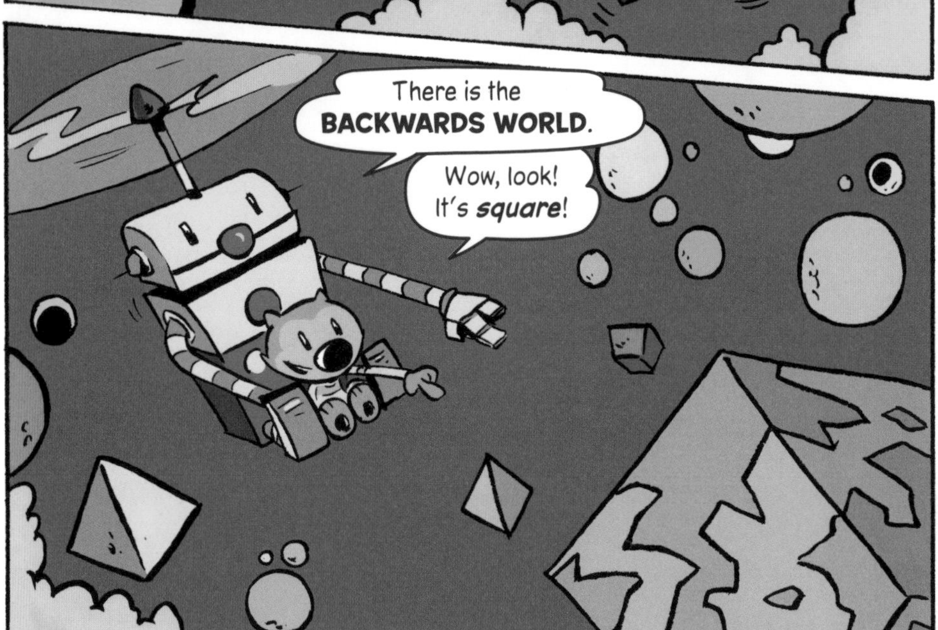
There is the
BACKWARDS WORLD.
Wow, look!
It's *square*!

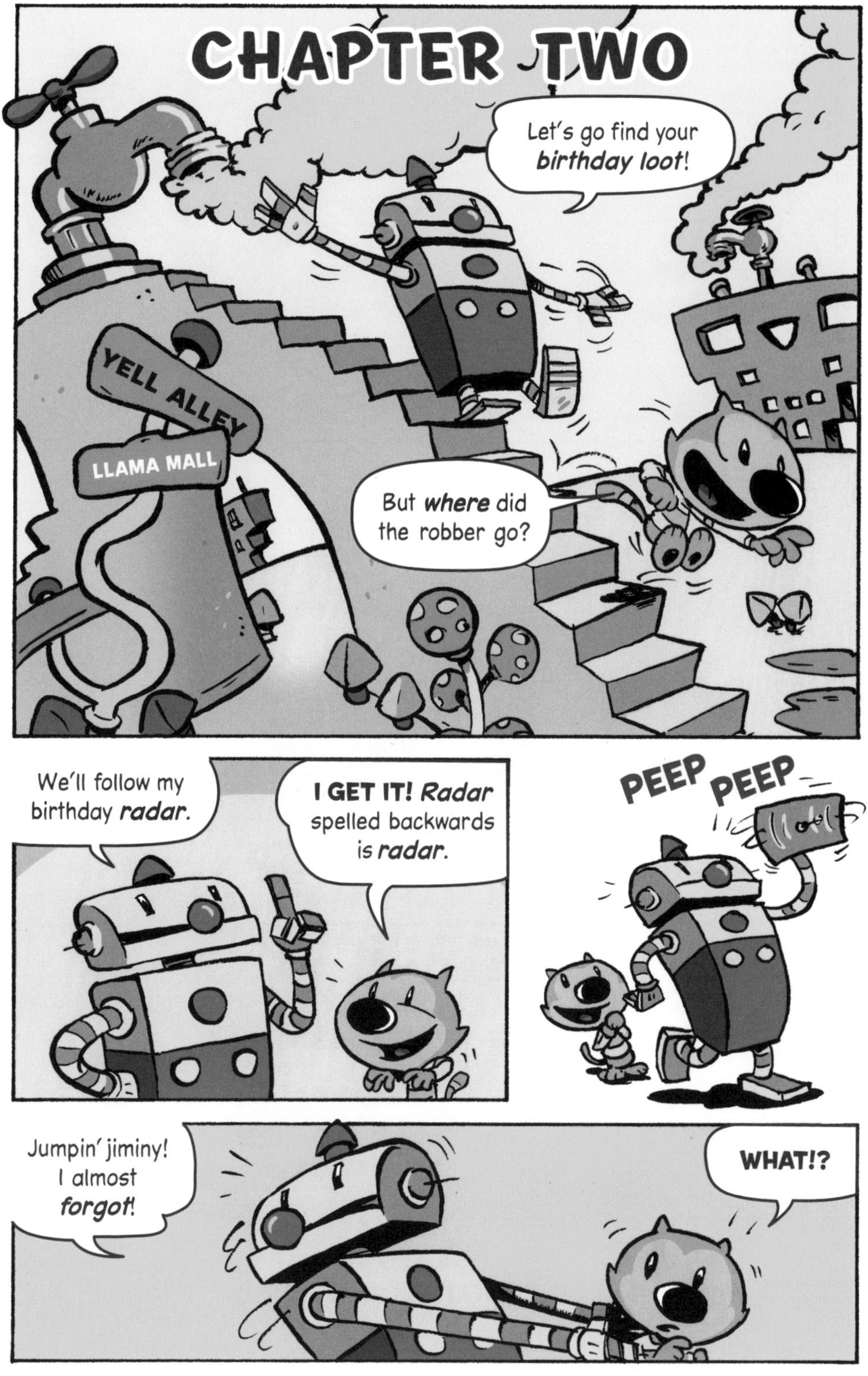
CHAPTER TWO
Let's go find your birthday loot!
YELL ALLEY
LLAMA MALL
But where did the robber go?
We'll follow my birthday radar.
I GET IT! Radar spelled backwards is radar.
PEEP PEEP
Jumpin' jiminy! I almost forgot!
WHAT!?

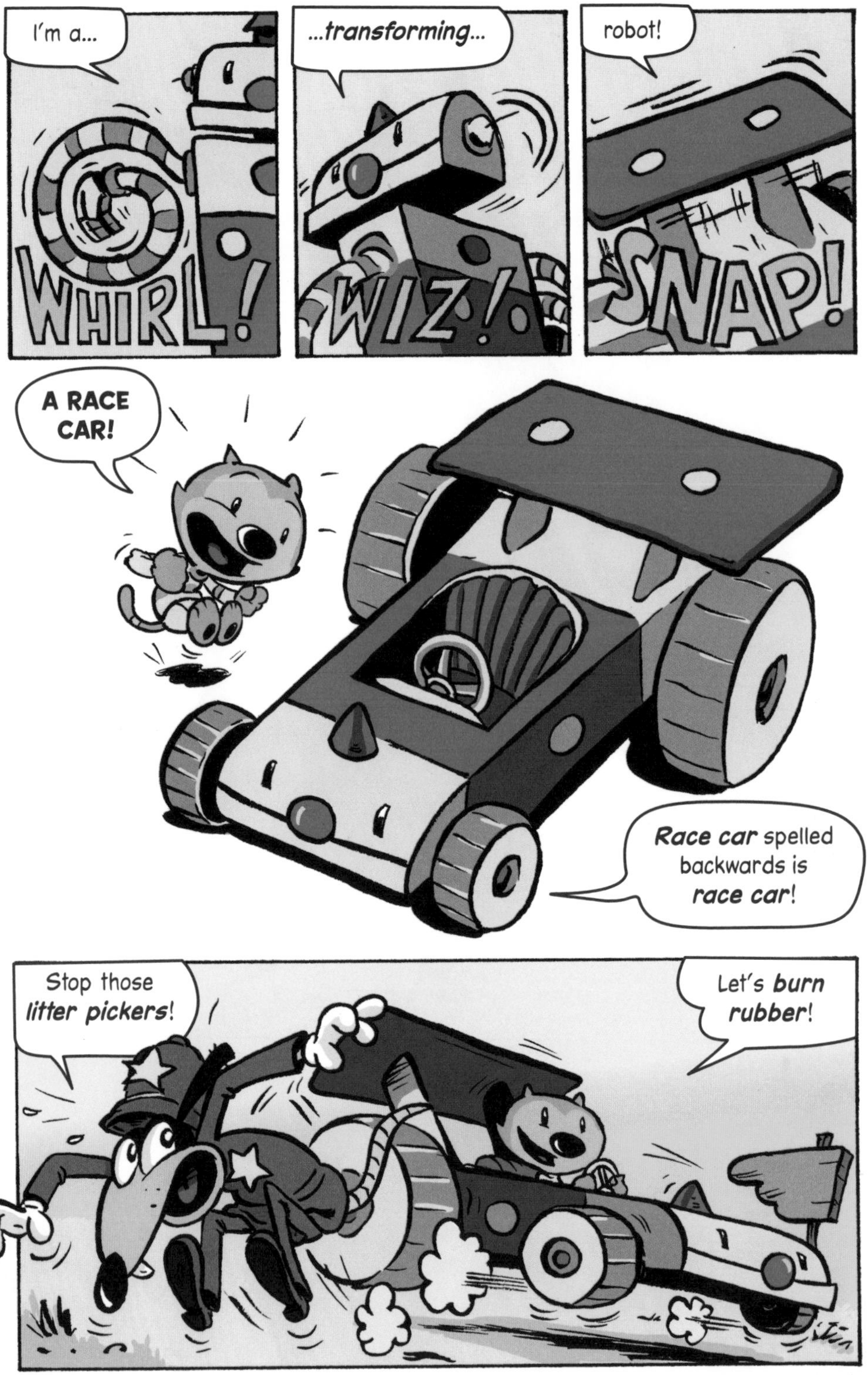
I'm a...
WHIRL!
...transforming...
WIZ!
robot!
SNAP!
A RACE CAR!
Race car spelled backwards is race car!
Stop those litter pickers!
Let's burn rubber!

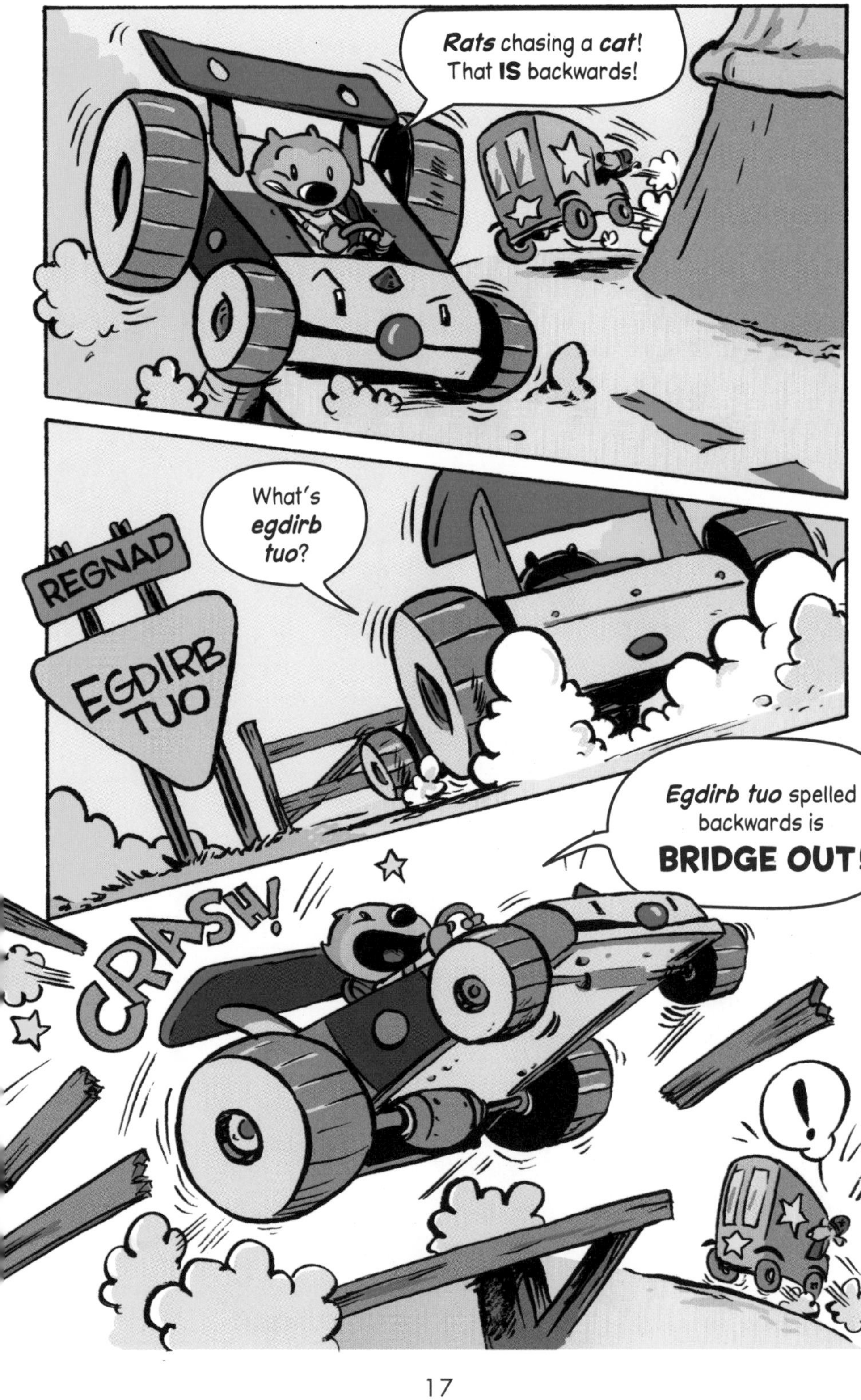
Rats chasing a *cat*! That **IS** backwards!
What's *egdirb tuo*?
REGNAD
EGDIRB TUO
Egdirb tuo spelled backwards is **BRIDGE OUT**!
CRASH!
!

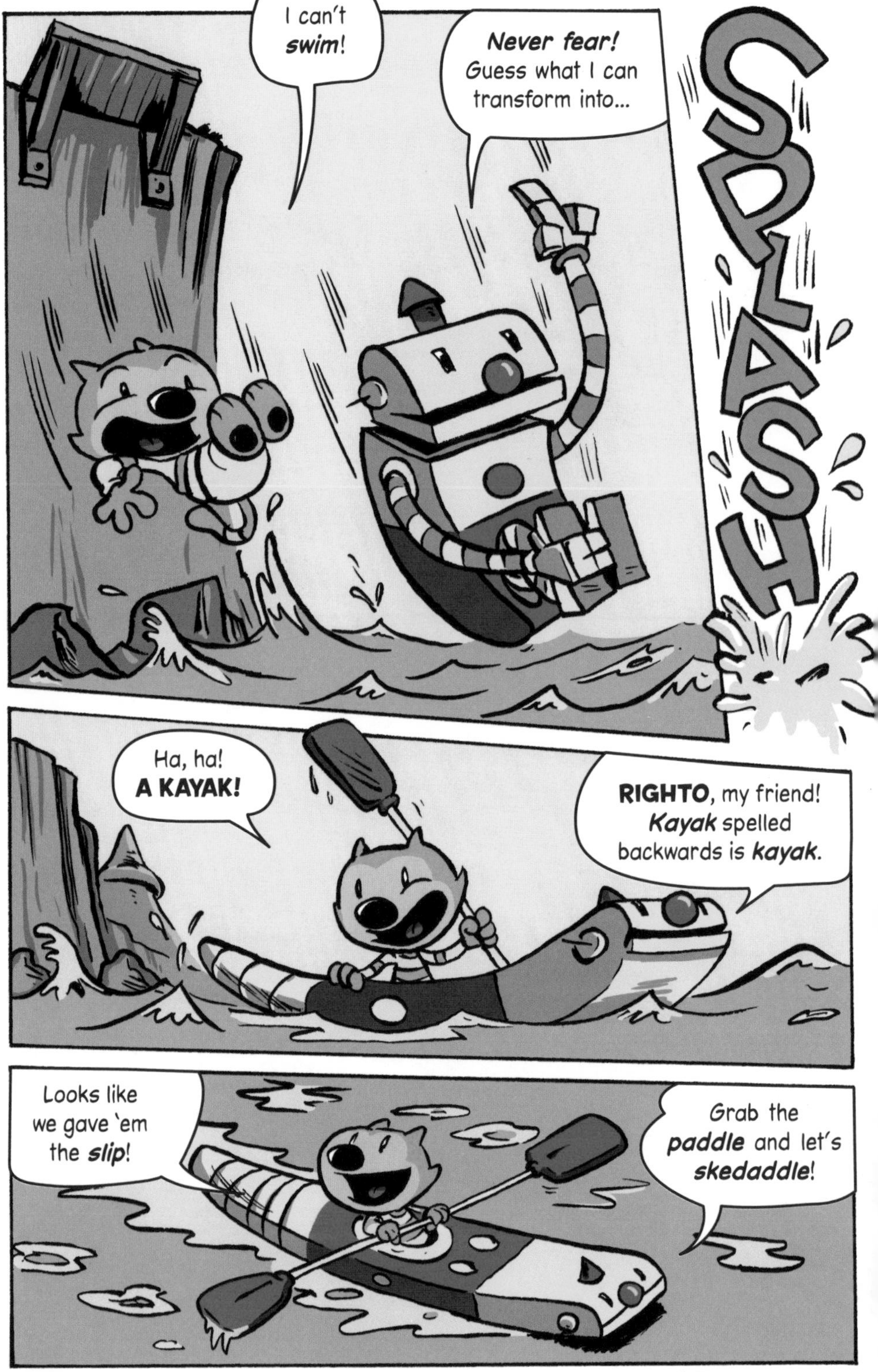
I can't *swim*!
Never fear! Guess what I can transform into...
SPLASH
Ha, ha! **A KAYAK!**
RIGHTO, my friend! ***Kayak*** spelled backwards is ***kayak***.
Looks like we gave 'em the ***slip***!
Grab the ***paddle*** and let's ***skedaddle***!

19

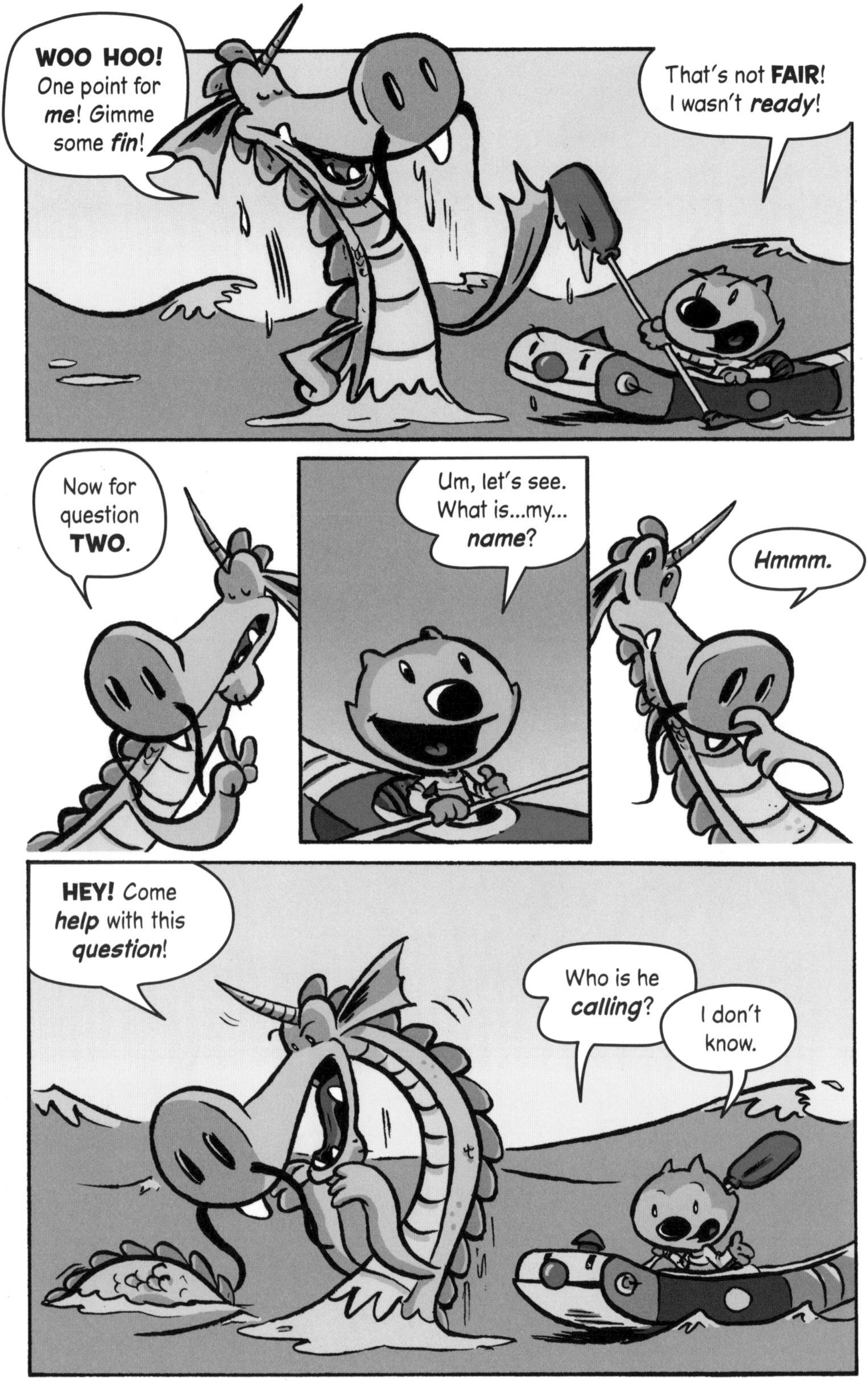
WOO HOO! One point for me! Gimme some fin!
That's not FAIR! I wasn't ready!
Now for question TWO.
Um, let's see. What is...my... name?
Hmmm.
HEY! Come help with this question!
Who is he calling?
I don't know.

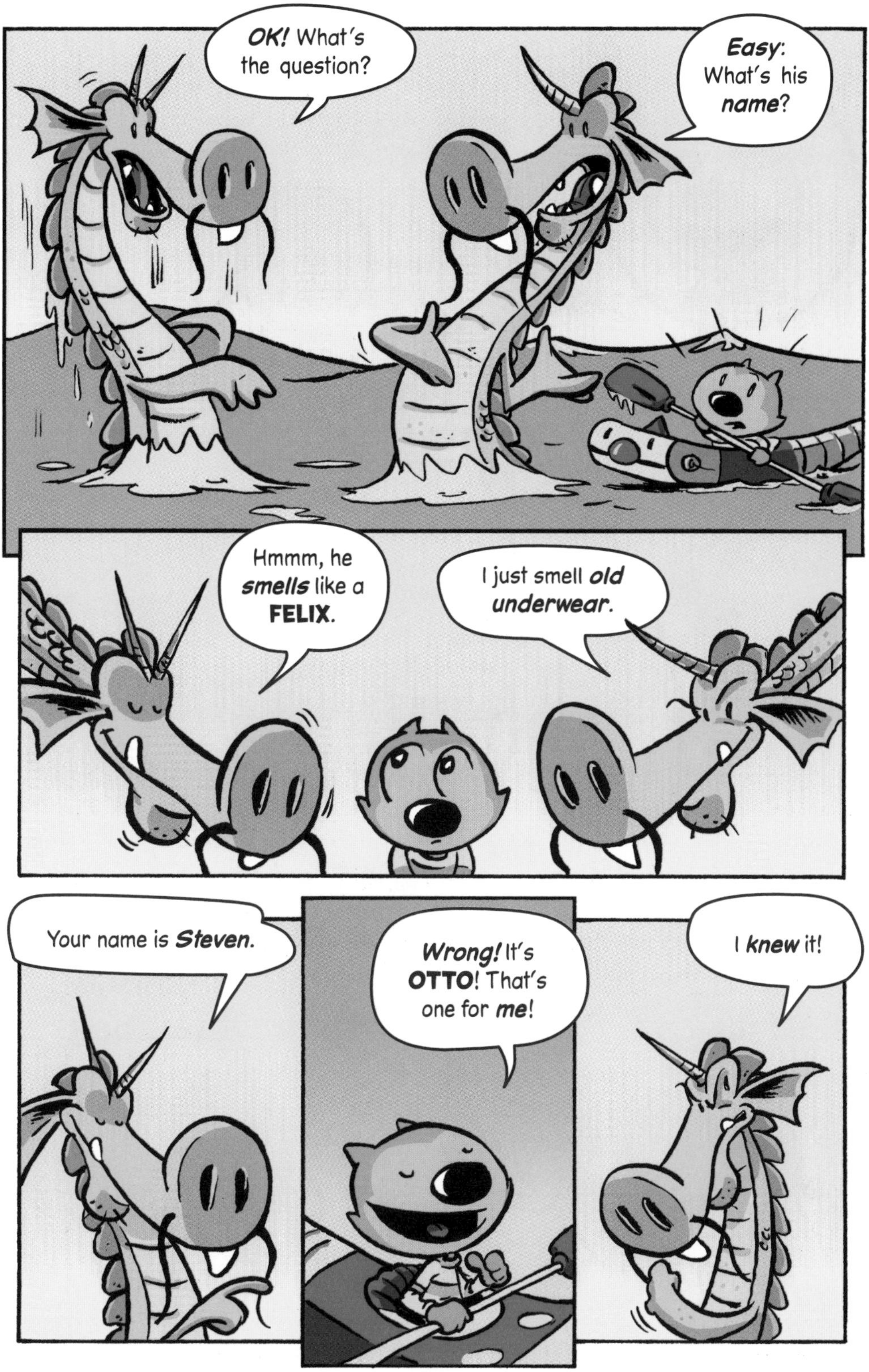
OK! What's the question?
Easy: What's his name?
Hmmm, he smells like a FELIX.
I just smell old underwear.
Your name is Steven.
Wrong! It's OTTO! That's one for me!
I knew it!

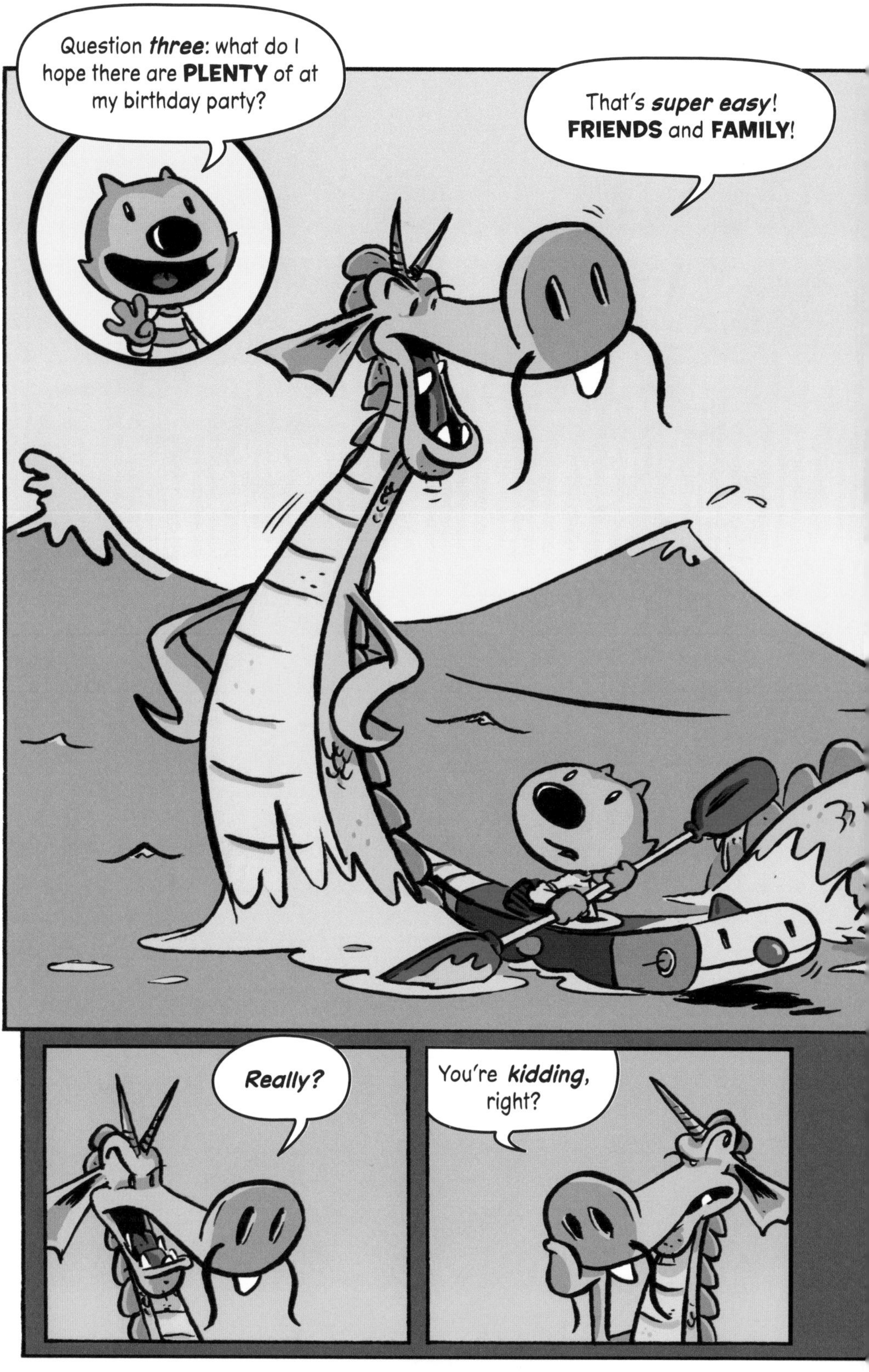
Question *three*: what do I hope there are **PLENTY** of at my birthday party?
That's ***super easy***! **FRIENDS** and **FAMILY**!
Really?
You're ***kidding***, right?

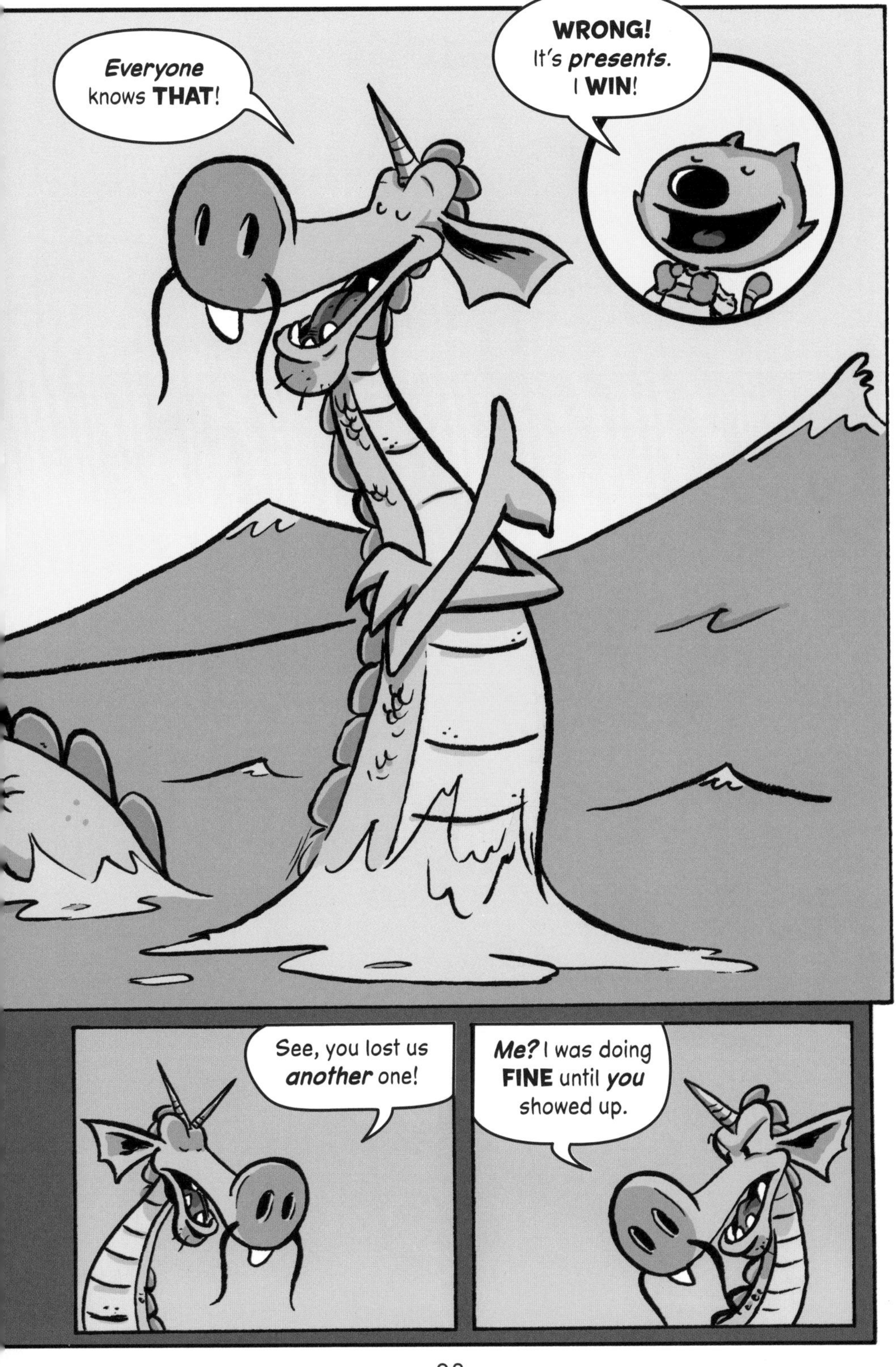
Everyone knows THAT!
WRONG! It's presents. I WIN!
See, you lost us another one!
Me? I was doing FINE until you showed up.

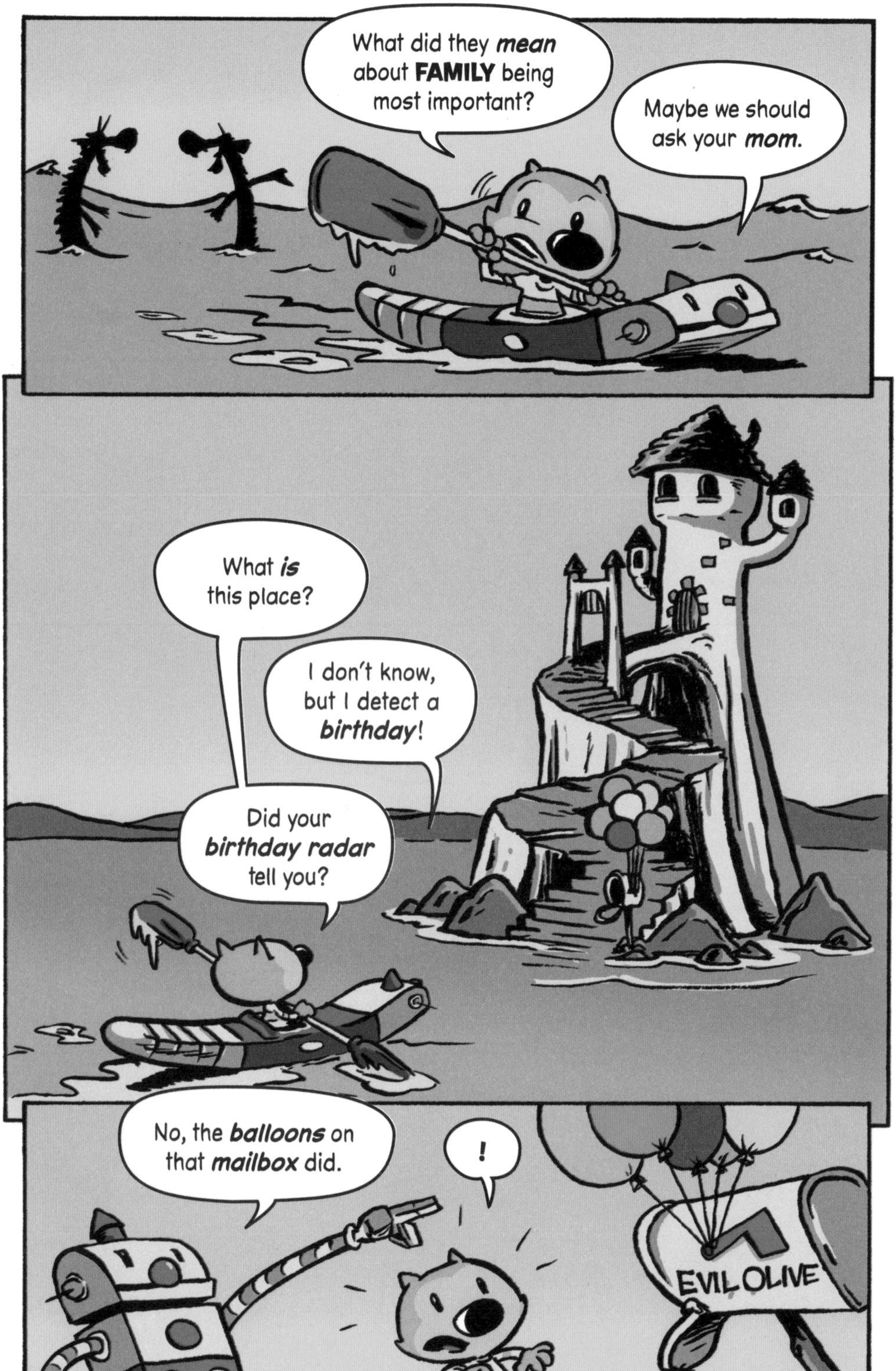
What did they *mean* about **FAMILY** being most important?
Maybe we should ask your *mom.*
What *is* this place?
I don't know, but I detect a *birthday*!
Did your *birthday radar* tell you?
No, the *balloons* on that *mailbox* did.
!
EVIL OLIVE

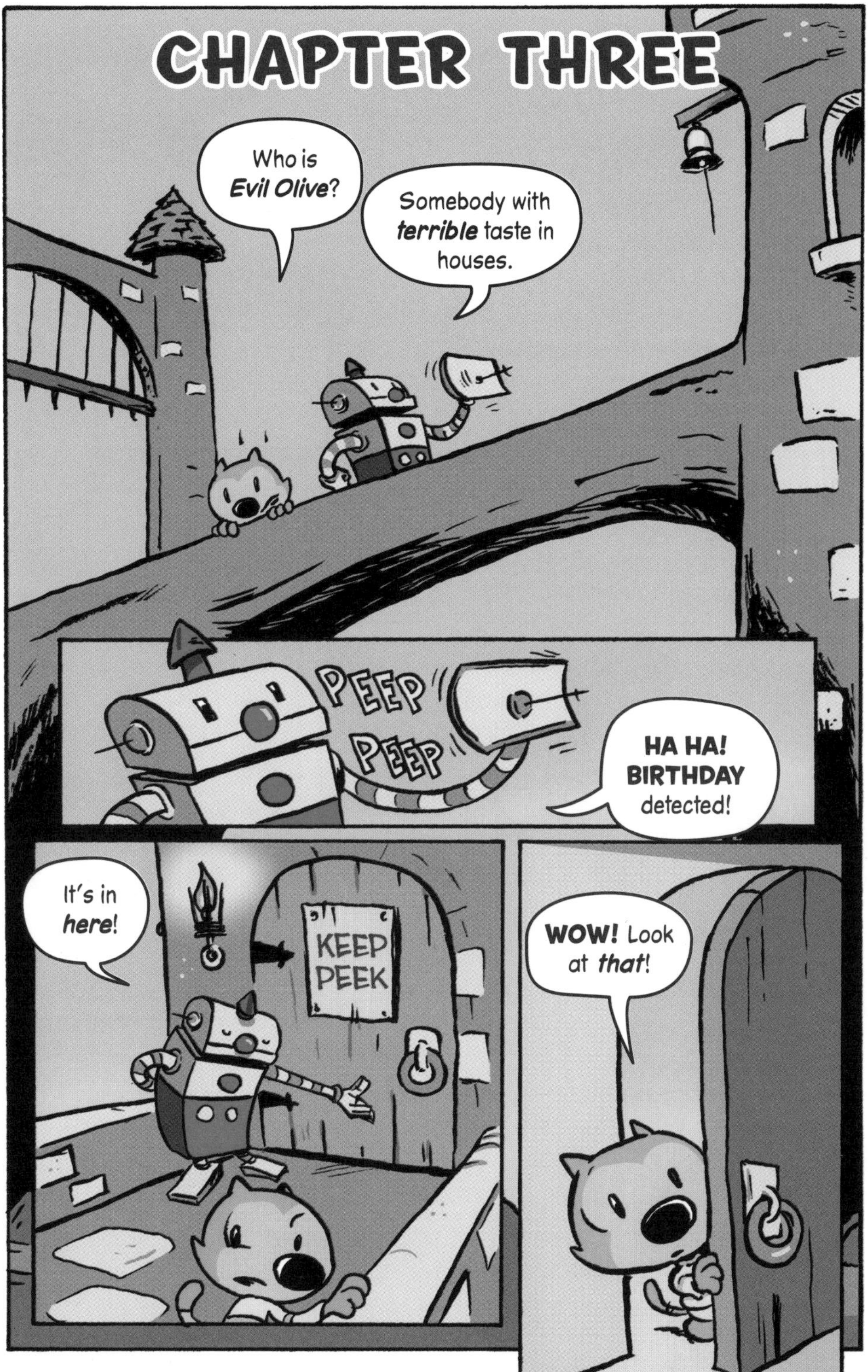
CHAPTER THREE
Who is *Evil Olive*?
Somebody with *terrible* taste in houses.
PEEP PEEP
HA HA! BIRTHDAY detected!
It's in *here*!
KEEP PEEK
WOW! Look at *that*!

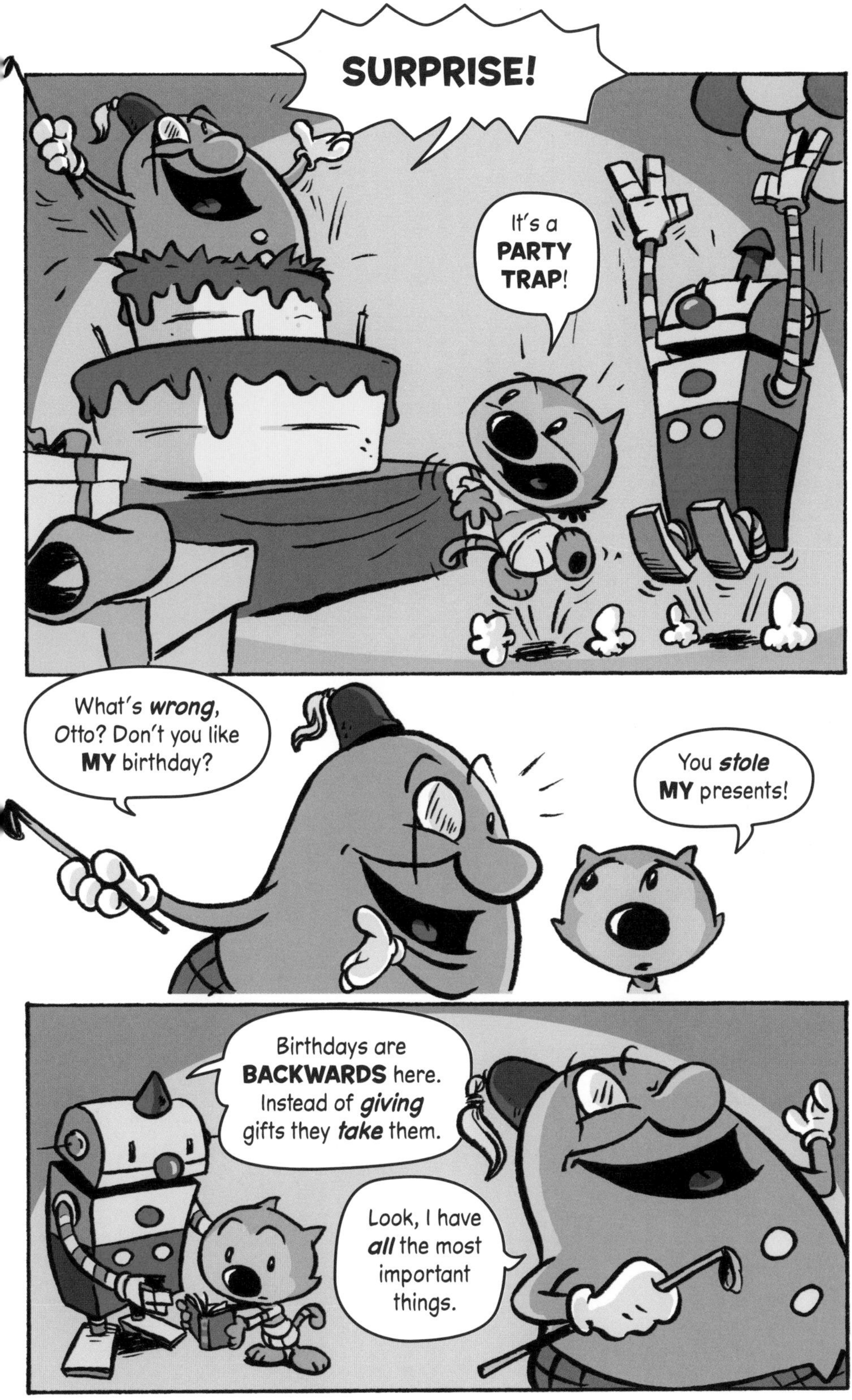
SURPRISE!
It's a **PARTY TRAP**!
What's ***wrong***, Otto? Don't you like **MY** birthday?
You ***stole*** **MY** presents!
Birthdays are **BACKWARDS** here. Instead of ***giving*** gifts they ***take*** them.
Look, I have ***all*** the most important things.

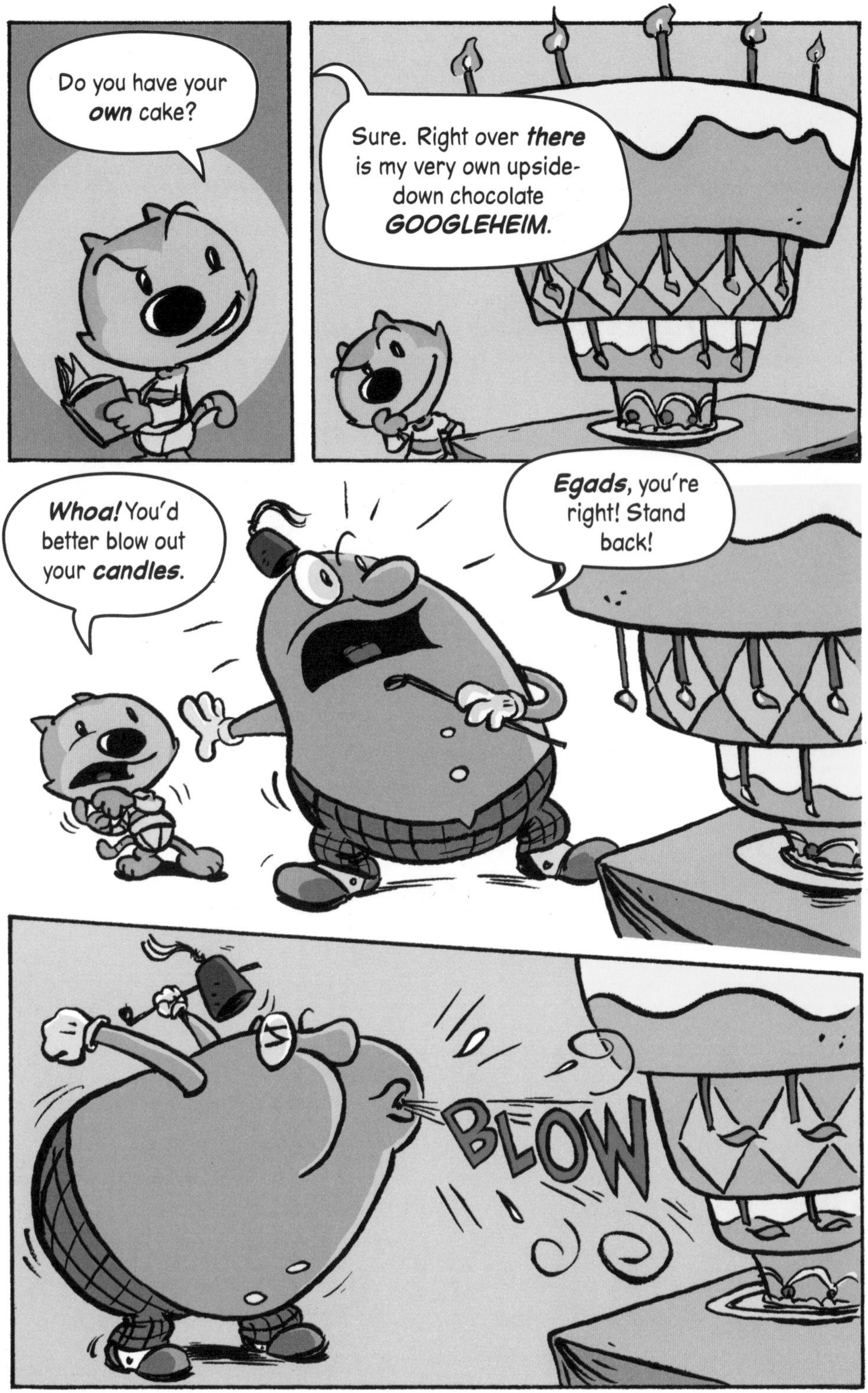
Do you have your *own* cake?
Sure. Right over *there* is my very own upside-down chocolate *GOOGLEHEIM*.
Whoa! You'd better blow out your *candles*.
Egads, you're right! Stand back!
BLOW

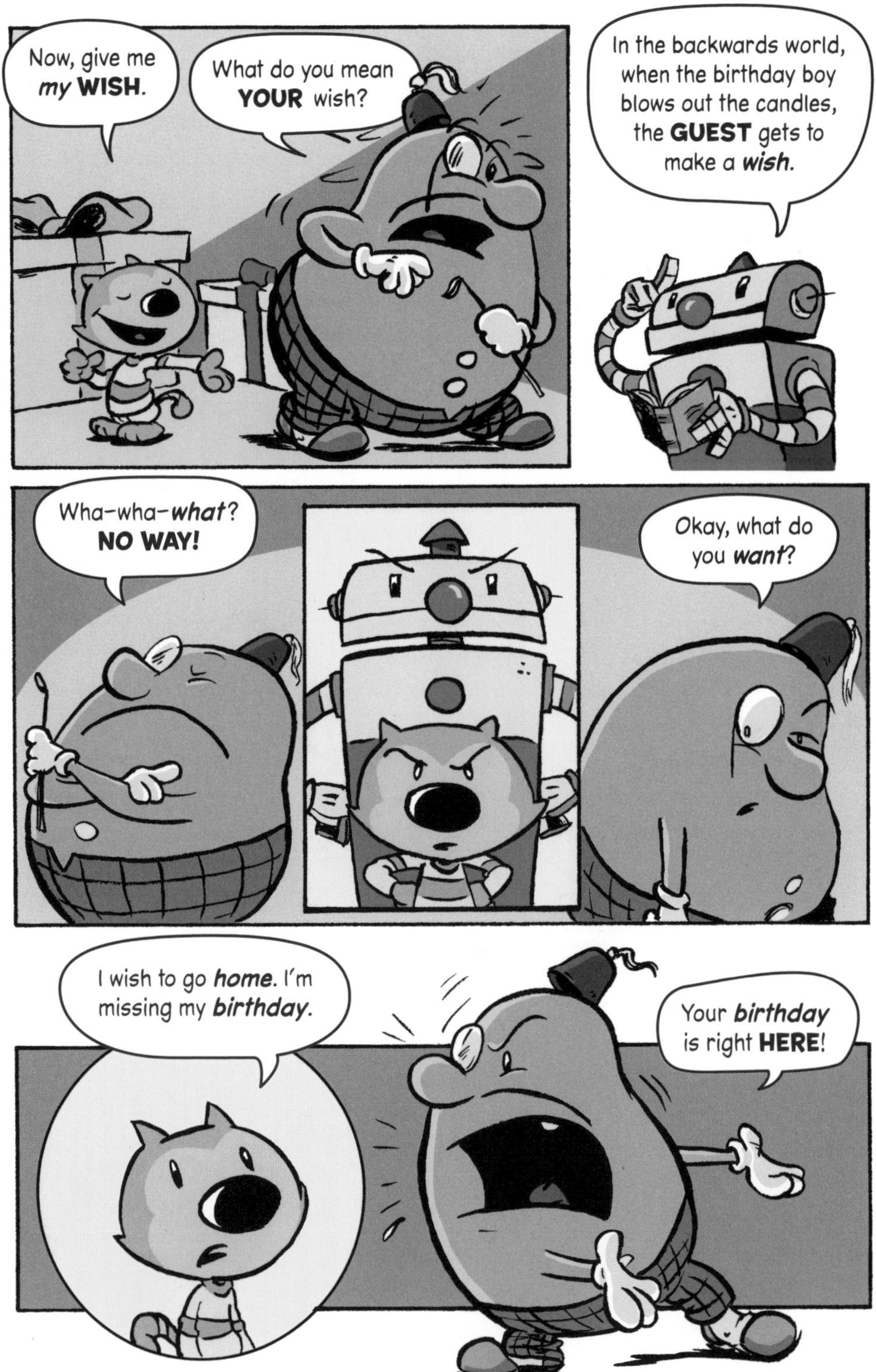
Now, give me *my* **WISH**.
What do you mean **YOUR** wish?
In the backwards world, when the birthday boy blows out the candles, the **GUEST** gets to make a ***wish***.
Wha-wha-***what***? **NO WAY!**
Okay, what do you ***want***?
I wish to go ***home***. I'm missing my ***birthday***.
Your ***birthday*** is right **HERE**!

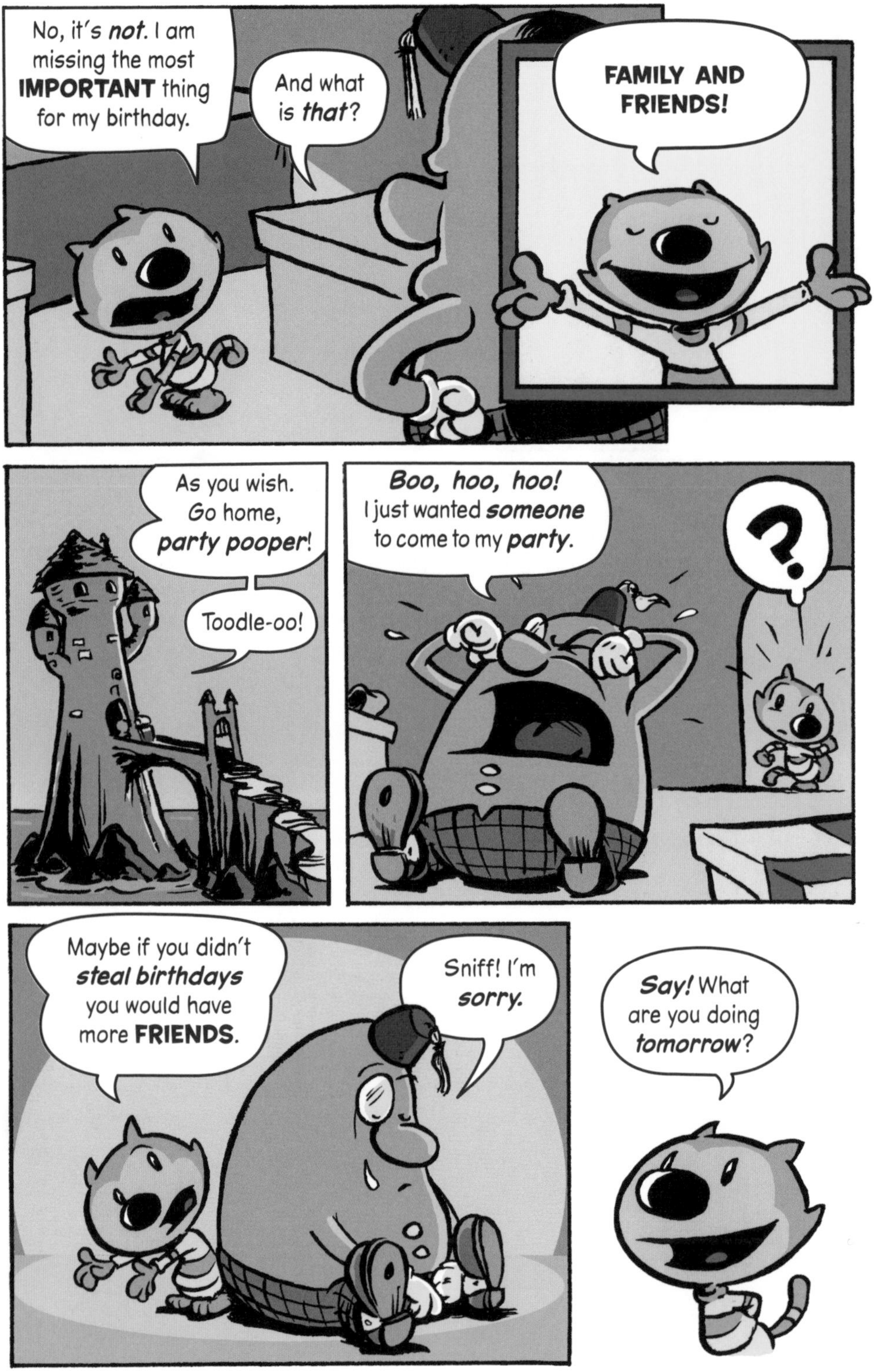
No, it's ***not***. I am missing the most **IMPORTANT** thing for my birthday.
And what is ***that***?
FAMILY AND FRIENDS!
As you wish. Go home, ***party pooper***!
Toodle-oo!
Boo, hoo, hoo! I just wanted ***someone*** to come to my ***party***.
?
Maybe if you didn't ***steal birthdays*** you would have more **FRIENDS**.
Sniff! I'm ***sorry.***
Say! What are you doing ***tomorrow***?

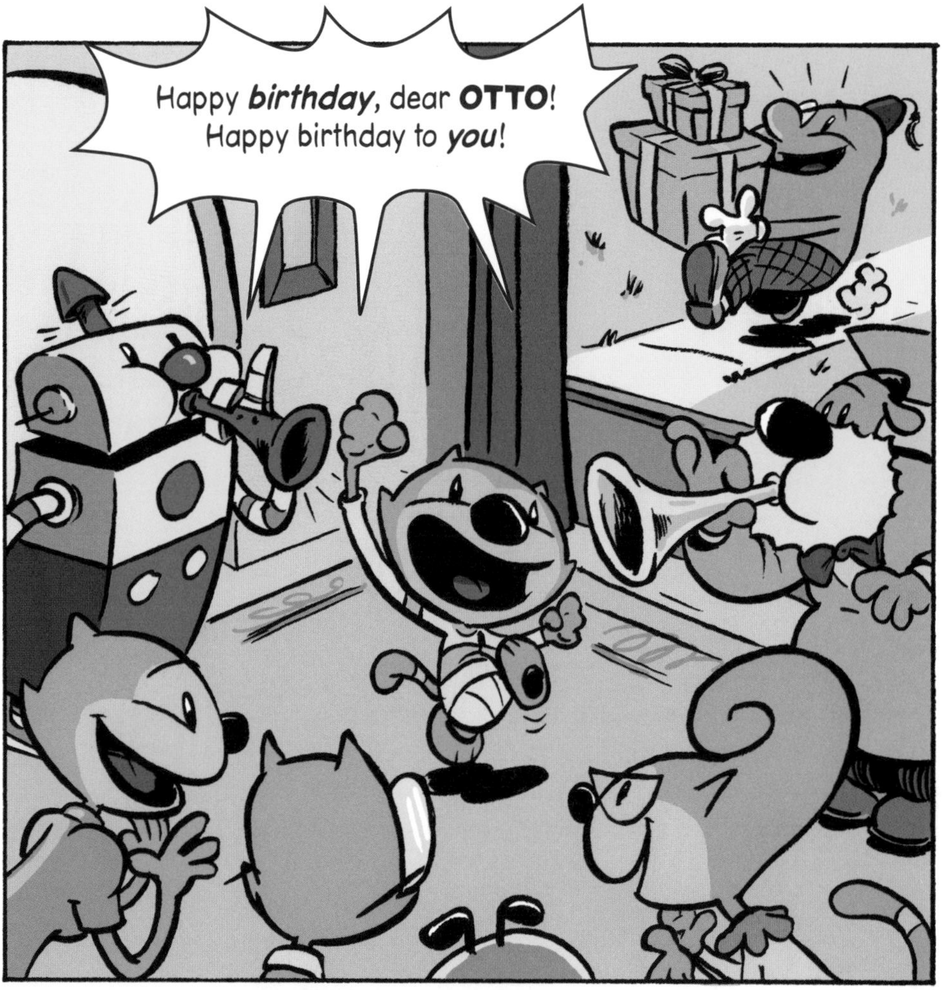
Happy *birthday*, dear **OTTO**!
Happy birthday to *you*!

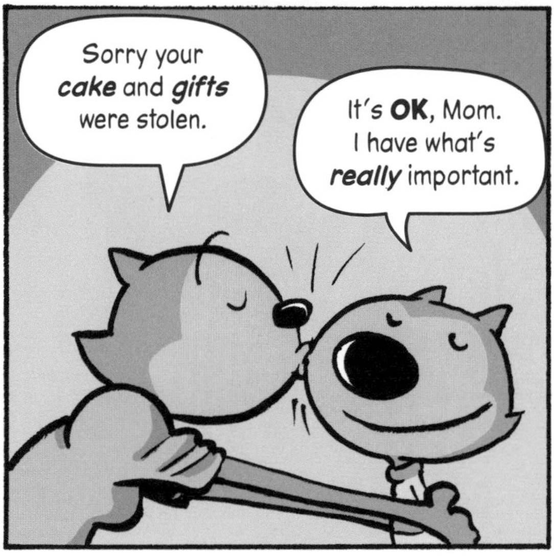
Sorry your *cake* and *gifts* were stolen.
It's **OK**, Mom. I have what's *really* important.

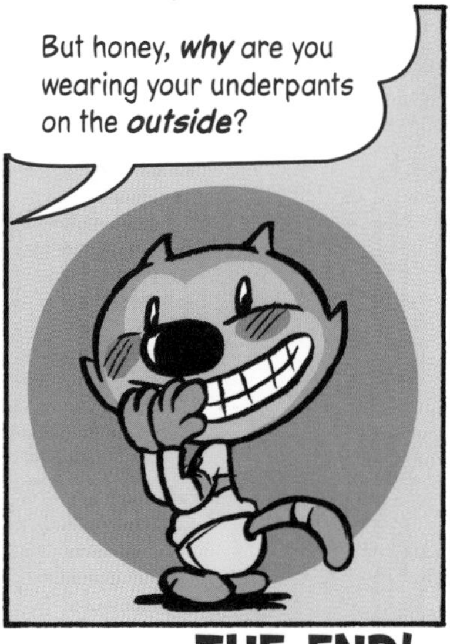
But honey, *why* are you wearing your underpants on the *outside*?

THE END!

ABOUT THE AUTHORS

FRANK CAMMUSO, who wrote and drew Otto's adventure, is the author of the graphic novel series *Knights of the Lunch Table*, a middle school version of King Arthur and his knights. His forthcoming series is *The Misadventures of Salem Hyde*. His writing has appeared in *The New Yorker*, *The New York Times*, *The Village Voice*, and *Slate*. **JAY LYNCH**, also a cartoonist, has helped create some of Topps Chewing Gum's most popular humor products, such as *Wacky Packages* and *Garbage Pail Kids*. Frank and Jay collaborated on the original TOON Book, *Otto's Orange Day*, which *School Library Journal* named a "Best New Book" and described as "a page-turner that beginning readers will likely wear out from dangerously high levels of enjoyment."

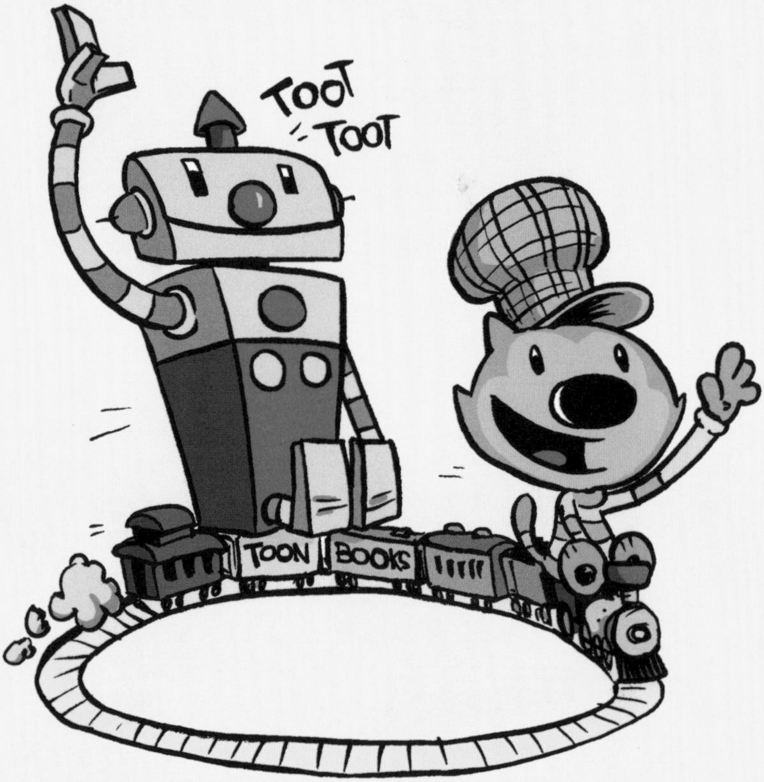
TOOT
TOOT
TOON
BOOKS

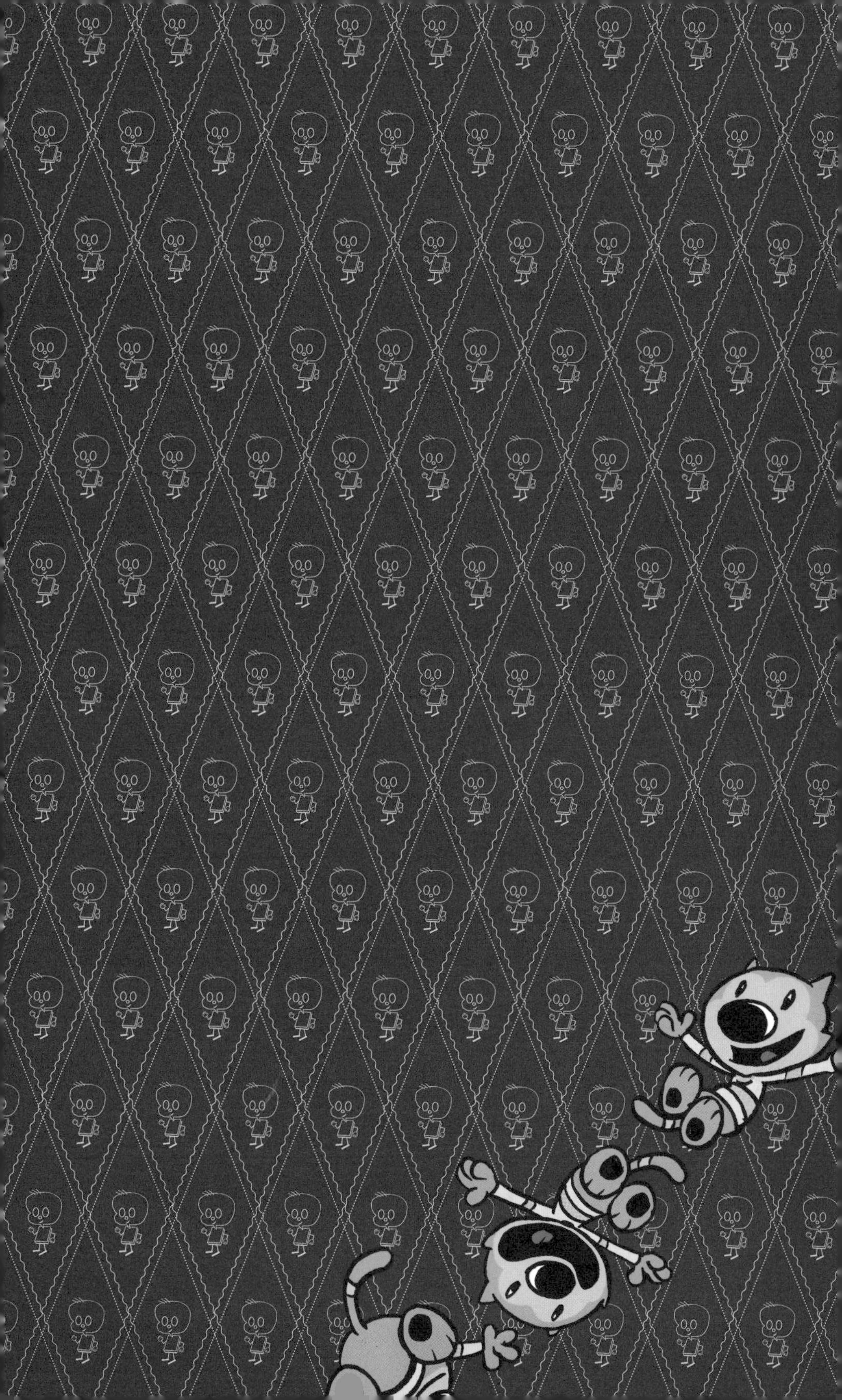

TIPS FOR PARENTS AND TEACHERS:

HOW TO READ COMICS WITH KIDS

Kids **love** comics! They are naturally drawn to the details in the pictures, which make them want to read the words. Comics beg for repeated readings and let both emerging and reluctant readers enjoy complex stories with a rich vocabulary. But since comics have their own grammar, here are a few tips for reading them with kids:

GUIDE YOUNG READERS: Use your finger to show your place in the text, but keep it at the bottom of the speaking character so it doesn't hide the very important facial expressions.

HAM IT UP! Think of the comic book story as a play and don't hesitate to read with expression and intonation. Assign parts or get kids to supply the sound effects, a great way to reinforce phonics skills.

LET THEM GUESS. Comics provide lots of context for the words, so emerging readers can make informed guesses. Like jigsaw puzzles, comics ask readers to make connections, so check a young audience's understanding by asking "What's this character thinking?" (but don't be surprised if a kid finds some of the comics' subtle details faster than you).

TALK ABOUT THE PICTURES. Point out how the artist paces the story with pauses (silent panels) or speeded-up action (a burst of short panels). Discuss how the size and shape of the panels carry meaning.

ABOVE ALL, ENJOY! There is of course never one right way to read, so go for the shared pleasure. Once children make the story happen in their imaginations, they have discovered the thrill of reading, and you won't be able to stop them. At that point, just go get them more books, and more comics.

www.TOON-BOOKS.c

SEE OUR FREE ONLINE CARTOON MAKERS, LESSON PLANS, AND MUCH MORE